Magic
Animal Friends

For Sienna Littley,
with love

Special thanks to Valerie Wilding

ORCHARD BOOKS

First published in Great Britain in 2014 by The Watts Publishing Group

8

Text © Working Partners Ltd 2014
Illustrations © Orchard Books 2014

A CIP catalogue record for this book is available from the British Library.

ISBN 978 1 40833 175 0

Printed in Great Britain by Clays Ltd, St Ives plc

The paper and board used in this book are made from wood from responsible sources

Orchard Books
An imprint of Hachette Children's Group
Part of The Watts Publishing Group Limited
Carmelite House, 50 Victoria Embankment, London EC4Y 0DZ

An Hachette UK Company
www.hachette.co.uk
www.hachettechildrens.co.uk

Poppy Muddlepup's Daring Rescue

Daisy Meadows

ORCHARD

Can you keep a secret? I thought you could!

Then I'll tell you about an enchanted wood.

It lies through the door in the old oak tree,

Let's go there now - just follow me!

We'll find adventure that never ends,

And meet the Magic Animal Friends!

Love

Goldie the Cat

Story One
A Tiny Feather

CHAPTER ONE: A Runaway Dog   9

CHAPTER TWO: The Flower Festival   25

CHAPTER THREE: Grizelda's Back   43

CHAPTER FOUR: Mrs Taptree's Library   53

CHAPTER FIVE: Honey Needlenose   61

CHAPTER ONE

A Runaway Dog

Light snow had just started to fall as Lily Hart spotted her best friend, Jess Forester, coming out of her house across the lane. She ran down the frosty garden path to meet her.

"I hope you're coming to help in the wildlife hospital!" she called, covering her

 9

dark bobbed hair with a woolly hat.

Jess laughed as she pulled her earmuffs over her blonde curls. "Of course I am," she said, checking the lane was clear. "You know I'd come every day if I could!"

The girls lived across the road from one another in the village of Brightley. Jess, her dad and Pixie the kitten shared a cottage, while Lily and her parents had a house with a large barn at the bottom of the garden. Mr and Mrs Hart had converted the barn into the Helping Paw Wildlife Hospital for sick and injured animals. Lily and Jess helped to care for the animals until they could be released

back into the wild.

"We've just rescued some baby

woodpeckers!" Lily

said, taking Jess

past the barn to

a new aviary. It

was a special

enclosure, with

room for birds

to fly around

inside. Mr Hart

was filling

a nest box

11

with wood chips, and Mrs Hart was crouched inside the aviary with a big basket.

She blew a strand of dark hair away from her eyes and grinned at them. "Hello, you two, these woodpecker chicks have hatched very late in the year. We're looking after them until they're grown. Would you like to introduce them to their cosy new nest box?"

"Yes, please!" Lily and Jess said, eagerly. They peered into the basket.

 12

The chicks flapped their black-and-white wings, chirping, "Kwick! Kwick!"

"Brrr, I'm going to make some hot chocolate," said Mrs Hart, standing up. "Come up to the house when you've settled them. You'll need warming up."

Once the nest box was ready, Jess and Lily gently lifted the tiny woodpecker chicks inside.

"Kwick, kwick!" they chattered.

"Can we watch them for a bit, Dad?" asked Lily. "We'll be very quiet."

"Of course," he replied. "Pop the lid back on when you've finished. We don't

13

want them getting snowed on!" He waved
goodbye as he followed Mrs Hart back to
the house.

The chicks used their long, pointed
beaks to poke about in the wood chips.

"They're trying to make a cosy hole to
sit in," said Lily. "Aren't they sweet?"

Suddenly, Jess heard barking. "It sounds
like there's a dog in the lane," she said.
"I wonder who it belongs to?"

Lily closed the nest-box lid and the
two girls ran to peer over the hedge.
A small brown dog was standing
underneath a pine tree. Its lead was

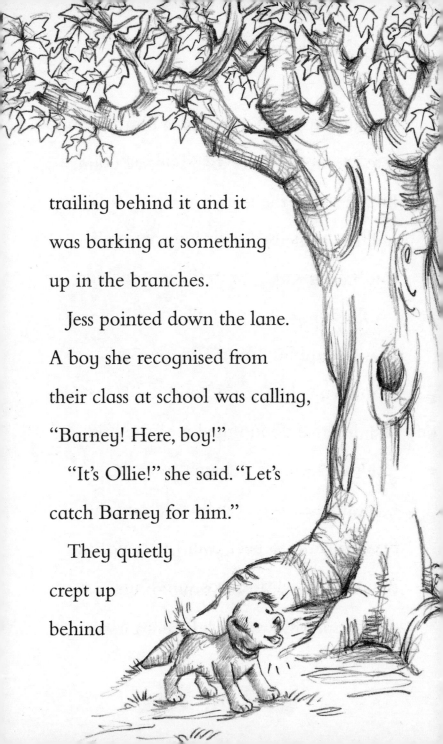

trailing behind it and it
was barking at something
up in the branches.

Jess pointed down the lane.
A boy she recognised from
their class at school was calling,
"Barney! Here, boy!"

"It's Ollie!" she said. "Let's
catch Barney for him."

They quietly
crept up
behind

the runaway dog. He was so busy staring

into the tree that he didn't notice them.

Lily grabbed the lead

and Jess ruffled Barney's

soft brown ears.

Ollie came

running up

to them.

"Thanks,

you two,"

he panted.

"Barney, you're so naughty." He tickled

the dog's chin. "Home time for you." As

they went off, Barney left neat puppy

paw-prints in the newly fallen snow,
alongside Ollie's welly-sized ones.

Jess started back to the wildlife hospital,
but stopped when she realised Lily was
still looking up into the pine tree. "What's
wrong?" she asked.

"I was wondering why Barney was
barking at the tree," said Lily. "Then
I thought I saw a flash of gold. . .Yes,
look!" she cried, pointing up to where a
beautiful green-eyed cat stepped lightly
along a branch towards her. "It's Goldie!"

The cat leaped into her arms, purring
and rubbing her head against Lily's chin.

The girls knew Goldie well. She was
a magical cat who lived in Friendship
Forest, a secret world full of talking
animals! Goldie had taken the girls on
four adventures there.

"We haven't seen you for ages, Goldie!"
Lily said. "We missed you."

Jess stroked the cat's golden fur.
"I wonder why she's come back here
today? Maybe Friendship Forest is in
danger again!"

Lily shuddered. "I hope not!"

The girls had worked with Goldie to
stop a nasty witch called Grizelda from

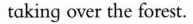

taking over the forest. At the end of their last adventure, the girls had made a new home in the swamp for Grizelda's servants, the Boggits. This had convinced the creatures to stop helping the witch with her plan to drive the animals out of their forest.

The cat jumped out of Lily's arms and turned towards the Harts' garden, miaowing loudly.

"She wants us to follow her," Jess

realised. "She must be taking us back to Friendship Forest!"

Excitement fluttered inside the girls as they hurried after Goldie. She led them past the wildlife hospital then towards Brightley Stream, which flowed at the bottom of the garden. The girls trod carefully on the stepping stones,

 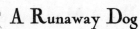

which were slippery with snow.

In the middle of the frosty meadow stood an oak tree. It looked bare and lifeless but, as they drew near, something magical started to happen ...

Suddenly, dark green leaves sprang from every branch, and scarlet berries gleamed in the winter sun. Red-breasted robins swooped from all

directions to chirrup sweetly in the high branches.

"Wow!" gasped Lily. "We've never seen it like this before, have we? There are snowflakes drifting around it, instead of butterflies and bees."

"It's as if it's put a winter coat on!" exclaimed Jess.

The purring cat stretched up a paw to touch the words that had magically appeared on the tree trunk.

"Ready?" Jess asked her friend.

Lily nodded, and together they read the words aloud. "Friend…ship…For…est!"

 22

A door, as high as the girls' shoulders, appeared in the trunk. In the centre was a leaf-shaped handle. When Jess opened it, golden light poured out, and Goldie sprang inside. Jess took Lily's hand and they ducked through into the shimmering, magical glow.

Both girls felt a familiar tingle, and knew that they were shrinking. When the glow faded, they found themselves in a sunlit forest clearing. Tall trees rustled in the warm breeze, and the familiar scent of candyfloss flowers filled the air.

"We're back in Friendship Forest!"

 23

said Lily. "And it's sunny!" She started
shrugging off her jacket. "I don't think
we'll need these warm clothes," she said
with a grin.

She added her earmuffs to the pile
of jackets, scarves, hats and gloves they
made in a hollow beside the tree. The girls
exchanged an excited glance. Now they
were back in Friendship Forest, who knew
what kind of adventure – and magic –
lay ahead?

CHAPTER TWO

The Flower Festival

"At last I can talk to you," sighed a soft voice happily.

Jess and Lily turned to see Goldie holding out her paws to them. She was standing upright, as tall as their shoulders now that they had shrunk, and wearing her golden scarf. Like all the Friendship

Forest creatures, she could talk.

"Oh, Goldie, it's lovely to be in Friendship Forest again!" cried Lily as the cat hugged them.

"Is that horrible witch, Grizelda, back?" asked Lily anxiously.

Goldie shook her head. "No," she said, "but I do need your help." She sat on a mossy tuffet and the girls settled down beside her.

"Do you remember that I was once a stray in the human world," Goldie began, "before I found my way here to Friendship Forest?"

Jess and Lily nodded.

"A young dog was very kind to me then," said Goldie. "You know him. He's called Barney."

"So that's why he was barking at the pine tree," said Lily. "He wasn't chasing you – he was excited to see you!"

"That's right," said Goldie. "And today is Barney's birthday, so I want to visit him. But every year, I judge the Friendship Forest Flower Festival, and guess what?"

"That's today, too?" asked Jess.

Goldie nodded. "Would you two take my place and be the festival judges?"

Lily's eyes shone. "Of course!" she said.

Jess was already on her feet. "I can't wait!" she said. "We'll see all our animal friends again!"

"Thank you," Goldie said, smiling. "I knew I could rely on you two. The

festival is in Sunshine Meadow. Come on,
I'll take you there!"

They followed Goldie through the
forest to Sunshine Meadow. Red, yellow
and orange flowers glowed brightly
among the grass. A long table was
set up in the middle, laid with shiny
prizes made by Agatha Glitterwing, the
magpie. Animals were setting out floral
arrangements on smaller tables dotted all
around the meadow.

Jess sniffed. "Those flowers smell so
gorgeous!" she said.

Just then, Woody Flufftail, a young

 29

squirrel, cried out, "Look, everyone!
Goldie's brought Jess and Lily!"

In a few moments, the girls were
surrounded by the friends they'd made
on their adventures in Friendship Forest.
Lucy Longwhiskers and the rest of her
rabbit family hopped up and down in

 30

excitement, while Ellie Featherbill the duckling quacked with joy.

Molly Twinkletail the mouse darted towards them. "You're back! You're back!" she squeaked. She was so little that Lily could scoop her up in one hand for a cuddle.

Bella Tabbypaw the kitten waved as she skipped over to them. "It's the girls! Hooray!" she cried, hugging Lily and Jess's legs.

"Hello, Bella!" said Jess, stroking the kitten's stripy head. The girls had helped rescue Lucy, Molly, Ellie and Bella from

31

Grizelda and her horrid helpers. It was lovely to see them safe and happy.

Goldie explained to Agatha, the festival organiser, that the girls were going to be the judges instead of her.

"Welcome, girls!" said Agatha, with a flap of her wings. "It's nice to meet you. Come on, everyone, let's get our flowers ready for the contest!"

The animals ran off, squealing and squeaking in excitement.

"I'll be back soon," Goldie told Lily and Jess as she hugged them goodbye. "Have a wonderful time!"

"Bye, Goldie!" they called. "Have fun with Barney!"

As well as the displays of flowers, some animals were running food stalls or organising games. Mrs Twinkletail, Molly's mother, gave them each a piece of cake from her stall.

"Yum," said Jess, taking a bite. "It tastes of roses! There are even sugared rose petals on the icing."

Lily pointed out a group of young animals who were using an enormous daisy chain as a skipping rope. "Look – everything at the festival involves flowers!"

Poppy Muddlepup

Jess noticed two puppies bounding between the stalls. They were as tall as the girls' knees and had very waggly tails. She and Lily hadn't met them before.

"They're so cute!" Jess whispered to Lily. Then she said to the puppies, "Hello! Who are you?"

"I'm Poppy Muddlepup," said one. Her fur was sandy-coloured and she wore a

red, heart-patterned bandana around her neck. She was holding a little bag with flowers peeking out of it. "This is my twin brother, Patch."

Patch looked just like Poppy, except for the brown patches in his sandy fur. His bandana was blue and was covered in stars instead of hearts.

"Goldie told us about you," said Patch, looking up at the girls. "We're glad you came, it's going to be so much fun!"

Across the meadow, Agatha Glitterwing jangled a bell.

"Ooh, it's time for the judging," said

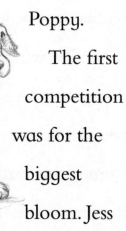

Poppy.
The first
competition
was for the
biggest
bloom. Jess
and Lily chose a pale yellow moonflower
as the winner. They were delighted to find
that it belonged to Captain Ace the stork.
He and his hot air balloon had helped
them rescue Molly Twinkletail.

Next, Jess and Lily measured the entries
for the tallest flower competition, and
gave the prize to Mr Silverback, the

badger, for his climbing dandyrose.

Molly Twinkletail and her nine brothers and sisters won a special award for their beautifully woven flower baskets. There were prizes for flower arrangements, and for the loveliest scent, and one for the best bouquet. The girls awarded the prize for the flowers with most petals to Poppy and Patch Muddlepup. Their red twisting twirls won easily. They had far too many petals to count!

"Would you like one?" Poppy asked. She picked a twisting twirl each for Lily and Jess. "You could put them in your

hair," she suggested shyly.

The long red flowers rustled softly, as if they were whispering.

"They're gorgeous," said Lily. "Are they hard to grow?"

"Not for us," said Patch. "We know lots about growing flowers. If you come to our family den in Garden Grove after the festival, we'll show you why."

Jess and Lily looked at each other. They'd love to spend more time with the puppy twins! "Great!" Jess cried.

Everyone cheered as they presented the rest of the prizes. When the festival came to an end, the girls said goodbye to their friends, and followed Poppy and Patch to Garden Grove. The two puppies were bouncing with excitement.

They led the girls into a sun-dappled clearing. A wooden den stood in the centre, surrounded by beds of strange and beautiful plants. Mr and Mrs Muddlepup came outside to greet the girls and admire the prize Poppy and Patch had won – a silver bowl. "Well done, you two!" said Mrs Muddlepup proudly.

Jess wandered over to a plant with long blue leaves and lemon-scented berries.

 39

She touched a leaf, then snatched her hand away. "It moved!" she cried.

The puppies rolled on the floor in laughter. "Our plants are magical," Poppy said. "Jess, touch the small curly plant with your shoe."

Jess did so, and both girls gasped when her white trainer turned pink.

"That's a colour clover. It makes things change colour," Poppy explained. "Watch the bubbling buttercup send out bubbles," she gabbled, "and just look at what the pompom puffball does." She blew on one of the purple flowers. The puffball

dissolved into bright pink smoke that
wafted away on the breeze.

"Wow!" said Lily. "These are fun!"

"They're helpful too," said Mr
Muddlepup. "We use them in potions to
make poorly animals feel better."

 41

Poppy held up her flower bag. "I always keep some with me, just in case I need them" she explained. "Come and see the rest of the garden!"

Jess was about to follow her when she spotted a familiar and very unwelcome sight. An eerie orb of yellow-green light was floating into Garden Grove. She nudged Lily.

"Oh no!" Lily whispered miserably. "Grizelda's back!"

CHAPTER THREE

Grizelda's Back!

"I wish Goldie was here," Lily whispered.
"We've never had to face Grizelda
without her help before."

"Well, we're going to have to now," Jess
said grimly.

They stood in front of the Muddlepups,
shielding them from the wicked witch.

 43

The orb of light grew bigger then…
Cra-ack! It exploded, spitting out angry
yellow-green sparks.

The sparks faded and revealed the
tall, thin witch. She wore a black cloak
over a shiny purple tunic and tight black
trousers. Long green hair swirled wildly
around her head. Her black boots had
high heels and sharply pointed toes.

"Ha!" she shrieked. "I might have
known you girls would be here.
Interfering, as usual! Clear off!"

"You clear off," Jess said bravely.

"There's nothing for you here,

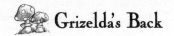

Grizelda!" said Lily.

Grizelda's laughter echoed around Garden Grove. "Nothing? Nothing?" she cackled. "I want those magical plants for a powerful potion, and I'm going to have them."

She reached for a bubbling buttercup, but Patch sprang in front of it and stood his ground, trembling.

"Yap! Yap! Grrr!" he barked.

Grizelda smiled a snarly smile, took a deep breath and blew.

Whooosh!

Patch was blown backwards by the witch's icy breath. He rolled over and over, yelping in fright.

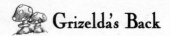

"Patch!" Mrs Muddlepup cried out. "Leave my puppy alone!"

Lily ran to scoop up the frightened puppy. He lay in her arms, shaking, as she comforted him.

"We won't let you take the plants from the Muddlepups!" Jess shouted at the witch. "We won't!"

Grizelda turned her gaze on Jess. "We'll see about that," she sneered. "I'm too clever for you."

She spread her cloak wide, looming over Patch and Lily. Her lips moved as she muttered to herself.

"She's casting a spell!" cried Jess. "Run, everybody!"

But it was too late. Lily felt Patch's little body sag in her arms. She looked down to see his eyes close as he fell into a deep, magical sleep.

"Oh no!" Lily glared at Grizelda. "What have you done?"

"Ha ha!" shrieked Grizelda. "You've got
until sunset to work it out. Give Garden
Grove and its magical flowers to me, or
the puppy will sleep... for ever. Haaa!"

Jess, Lily and the Muddlepups gazed in
horror as the witch snapped her fingers,
and disappeared in an explosion of
spitting yellow sparks.

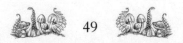

Mrs Muddlepup ran to Lily and, together, they laid Patch down on a soft cushion of moss. His paws twitched and he made a little snuffling sound before starting to snore softly.

"Wake up, Patch," his mother urged, gently shaking him.

Poppy lifted one of her brother's ears and called, "Wakey wakey!"

Mr Muddlepup fetched a hazelnut cracker and held it under the puppy's nose. "It's his favourite," he explained.

But Patch just kept snoring.

"Let's take him inside," Lily said, and carried him indoors. Mrs Muddlepup made a soft, cosy nest of blankets for her to lie him in.

"We must wake up Patch," Jess said. "But we can't let Grizelda have Garden Grove either. If we're going to stop her wicked plan, we have to work out a way to wake him up on our own."

"But how?" Lily wondered out loud.

"What should we do?"

"I wish Goldie was here!" Jess frowned.

They were both thinking hard, when Poppy tugged on Lily's sleeve.

"Ask Mrs Taptree!" said the puppy. "She's got books about everything in her library. Me and Patch borrow them all the time."

Lily and Jess grinned.

"My dad says you can always find help in a book," said Jess. "That's a brilliant idea, Poppy!"

CHAPTER FOUR

Mrs Taptree's Library

Lily and Jess told Mr and Mrs Muddlepup
where they were going. To their delight,
Poppy insisted on coming too. She led
them on a long walk through the forest.
At last, they reached the hollowed-out
trunk of a chestnut tree. Inside, they could
hear the tap-tap-tap of a woodpecker.

"This is Mrs Taptree's library," Poppy said.

"I can't believe that at home we were looking after some woodpeckers," Lily murmured excitedly, "and now we're about to talk to one!"

From inside the hole in the tree, a high voice squawked, "Come in! Books for all in my library! Quick! Quick!"

"How is there room for a library in

 54

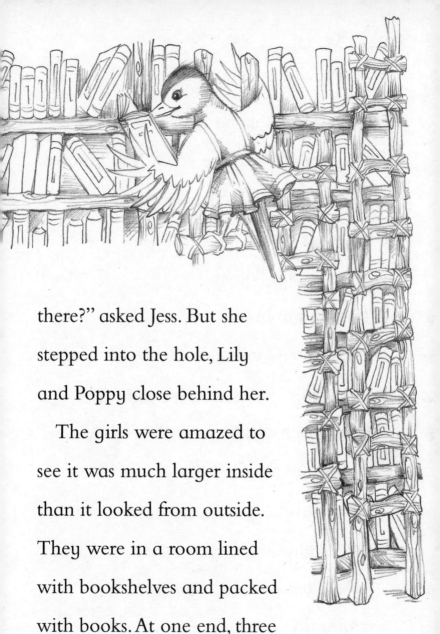

there?" asked Jess. But she stepped into the hole, Lily and Poppy close behind her.

The girls were amazed to see it was much larger inside than it looked from outside. They were in a room lined with bookshelves and packed with books. At one end, three ladders stood, side by side.

"Welcome!" said the voice. Mrs Taptree
the woodpecker fluttered down
from the top shelf.
"Hello, young Poppy.
What kind of book
are you three looking
for today?"

Poppy introduced
the girls and they
all explained
about Patch.

"Dear me,
we must do

something," said Mrs Taptree. "We're sure to find an answer in one of my books. Let's look." She clapped her wings and said, "Ladders!"

Instantly, the ladders magically slid along the bookshelves.

"Wow!" said Jess.

"Just say left or right, up or down, or even, 'Find a book about bees,'" said Mrs Taptree. "The ladders will take you where you want to go."

They began searching. Poppy examined the books along the bottom shelf, and the girls stepped onto the ladders.

 57

"Left!" said Lily, and slid to the plant
section.

"Magic books, please," Jess called,
grinning as her ladder whizzed along

Suddenly, two young woodpeckers burst
in, wings flapping. "Mum! Quick! Quick!

Can we have a chestnut cake, please, can
we?" said one. Then he saw Jess and Lily.
"Ooh, what are those?"

"They're girls," said Mrs Taptree. "Lily

 58

and Jess, these are my chicks, Dig and
Tipper. If you two go out to play while
I help the girls find a book, I'll give you
a cake when we've finished. Off you go,
chicks, quick, quick!"

"All right, Mum," said Dig, running out.
But Tipper knocked over a pile of books
as she flapped past.

Lily stepped over to pick them up. "Hey,
Jess!" she said, opening one. "This is about
magic potions." She flicked through it,
then yelled, "I think I've found something!
A recipe for Rise and Shine potion. It
says, 'Guaranteed to wake sleepers from

even the deepest slumber'."

"Fantastic!" said Jess.

Poppy's soft brown eyes looked anxiously at the girls. "Can we use it to wake Patch?"

Lily hugged her. "Of course. All we have to do is find the right ingredients!"

CHAPTER FIVE

Honey Needlenose

"Right, what ingredients do we need?" asked Jess eagerly.

Lily read the recipe. "A tiny feather the colour of sunlit leaves, some jewel water, and… Oh dear, I can't read the last thing. It's smudged." She looked up. "Now what? We don't know the third ingredient!"

 61

Jess shrugged. "Let's find the first two," she said. "Maybe someone can help us work out what the missing one is."

"A tiny feather…" murmured Lily.

"The colour of sunlit leaves," said Jess.

Poppy's ears perked up. "Like a hummingbird's!" she cried. "They have teeny tiny feathers, all the colours of the rainbow."

Lily dropped a kiss on the puppy's head. "Clever Poppy!" she said. "But where will we find a hummingbird?"

Mrs Taptree flapped her wings. "Look for crimson bell flowers and you'll find a

hummingbird," she said. "They can't smell
the marshmallow scent, but they adore
the colour – and the nectar."

Poppy darted to the door. "I'll soon sniff
out that marshmallow scent!" she cried.

The girls thanked Mrs Taptree then
hurried out of the library and after the
puppy as she bounded through the forest,
sniffing loudly.

"Here!" Poppy cried, snuffling beneath
a holly tree. "Oh no, it's only jellyberries."

"Jellyberries?" said Lily.

"Mmm," said Poppy. "You drop them
in water and in seconds you have a bowl

of yummy pink jelly." She picked a few and put them in her bag. "Patch loves jelly," she explained. She looked sad for a moment. "I'll make it for him when he wakes up." Then she sniffed again and dashed past a clump of nettles. She slid to a stop before a curtain of vines.

"Yap! They're here!" she called. "And they smell delicious!"

Jess parted the vines, revealing a cluster of brilliant red flowers, nodding their bell-like heads. She put a finger to her lips. A tiny green-and-blue bird, scarcely longer than her little finger, darted in and out of the flower bells. Its wings flapped so fast they were a colourful blur.

"Beautiful," breathed Lily. "Um, hello? Miss Hummingbird?" she called softly.

The bird dived beneath the flowers' broad leaves anxiously.

"We won't hurt you," said Jess. "Mrs Taptree the woodpecker said you might be able to help us."

The leaves quivered.

"Oh dear, she's nervous," said Jess. "We'll have to coax her out." She looked at the red twisting twirl in Lily's hair. "Mrs Taptree said hummingbirds like red – maybe we can tempt her out with the flowers Poppy gave us?"

Honey Needlenose

Lily nodded. The girls held out their
twisting twirls, while Poppy talked quietly.
"Please come out," she said. "Jess and Lily
are girls. They're good and kind."

A long pointed beak appeared, followed
by bright little eyes. "Are you sure?" said
the hummingbird, in a high, sweet voice.

"I'm sure," said Poppy.

The hummingbird darted out. "Hello.
I'm Honey Needlenose," she said shyly.

"Hello, Honey," said Lily. "We need
your help to save Poppy's brother." She
explained about the potion and the
first ingredient. "So you see, if we don't

manage to wake him up ourselves, the Muddlepups will have to give up Garden Grove to that horrible witch."

"I'll gladly give you a feather," said Honey. "I just dropped one. There!" She dived down, picked up a shimmering green feather in her thin beak, and let it fall onto Lily's hand.

"Wow!" said Lily. "It's so tiny! And it's definitely the colour of sunlit leaves."

"Thank you, Honey," said Jess.

"Thank you for the twisting twirls," the hummingbird replied, and went back to gathering nectar.

Lily gave the feather to Jess, who tucked it safely between the pages of the notebook she always kept in her pocket.

"We've found the first ingredient!" said Lily, grinning.

Poppy yapped happily and bounded around at the girls' feet. "Hooray, hooray!" she cried. "We're going to save Patch!"

Jess picked up the little puppy and swung her into the air. "Yes, we will," she said. "Thanks to your clever nose, we're off to a fantastic start. Well done, Poppy! Now we just have to find the rest of the ingredients for the Rise and Shine potion."

"With Poppy's nose on the case, I'm sure we'll be waking Patch up in no time," said Lily. "Come on, you two, let's get searching!"

The three friends set off back through the forest, determined to save Patch and Garden Grove.

 70

Story Two
Jewel Water

CHAPTER ONE: A Mysterious Girl   73

CHAPTER TWO: A Thorny Trick   83

CHAPTER THREE: Desperate for Help   93

CHAPTER FOUR: Bottle Blooms   103

CHAPTER FIVE: The Treasure Tree   109

A Mysterious Girl

It was mid-afternoon in Friendship Forest.
Lily Hart and Jess Forester were sitting
on a fallen tree trunk, deep in thought.
Poppy Muddlepup the puppy was flopped
beside them on a heap of crisp, dry beech
leaves. The three friends had already
collected the tiny feather they needed for

 73

the Rise and Shine potion that would

wake Poppy's twin brother Patch from

his magical sleep. But they still needed to

find some jewel water – and they didn't

even know what the third ingredient was.

They only had until sunset to succeed. Otherwise, Grizelda the witch would take over Garden Grove from the Muddlepup family, and use the magical flowers there to make nasty potions.

"We've been hunting for jewel water for ages," said Jess, "but it's no good. I don't even know what it's supposed to be!"

Poppy's ears drooped sadly.

Lily frowned. "Come on. It's got to be here somewhere. We've seen jewels once before in Friendship Forest, haven't we? I think we saw some during our adventure with Bella Tabbypaw."

Poppy's ears pricked up. "Where? What happened?" she asked.

Lily explained that Grizelda's smelly servants, the Boggits, had taken Bella to a cavern beneath Toadstool Glade. When Lily, Jess and Goldie had followed them, they had seen jewels in the roof.

"But, Lily," said Jess, "there wasn't any water in the cavern. I don't see how there could be any jewel water there."

Poppy's ears drooped again.

"But if there are jewels in the cavern under Toadstool Glade," Lily said slowly, "maybe there are jewels somewhere around the glade itself too. There are little streams all over the forest, aren't there?"

"So maybe jewel water comes from a stream that has jewels lying inside it," finished Jess, her eyes shining. "Yes, it's worth a try. Let's go!"

They hurried off towards Toadstool Glade, Poppy trotting beside them.

"We should move as quietly as possible," Jess said as they drew near, "so we can listen for running water."

She led the way along a narrow path. On either side, tall trees loomed over nut bushes and clumps of curly ferns.

 77

"Stop!" Poppy whispered suddenly. "I heard a voice." Her ears were pricked up, listening. "Someone's singing."

Lily and Jess cautiously rounded a large shrub and almost bumped into a girl about their age. She had a sweet, smiling face and wore a pink flowery dress and strappy pink sandals. Her long wavy hair was the colour of marmalade.

"Er, hello!" said Jess, shocked. She glanced at Lily. Goldie had told them that they were the only humans who visited Friendship Forest!

"Hello," said the girl. "You look nice.

 78

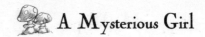

And what a dear little doggie." She bent to

pat Poppy. "Oh, you cute little puppy!"

Poppy glanced up at Jess and Lily. She

seemed unsure, so Jess said, "Don't be shy."

The puppy's tail gave a small wag.

Lily asked the girl, "Excuse me, but –
are you human? Like us? We didn't think
anyone else came here."

"Mmm," said the girl. "I live not far
away." She waved her arm vaguely. "I'm
visiting the pretty forest, too."

"I'm Jess, and this is Lily," said Jess.
"And this is Poppy Muddlepup, our friend.
What's your name?"

"Oh, er, my name's… Gretchen," said
the girl. "Gretchen, that's it." She moved
closer. "I couldn't help overhearing you
say you're looking for jewel water."

"Oh?" said Lily eagerly. "Do you know

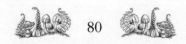

80

where some is?"

"Yes," said Gretchen. "I'll take you there. On the way you can tell me why you want it. Come on!"

Jess and Lily looked at each other, thrilled. They were going to have everything they needed to break Grizelda's spell in no time!

"That's great, Gretchen, thanks," said Lily. "It was lucky we bumped into you!"

"Yes, it was, wasn't it?" said Gretchen. She looked very pleased too.

Poppy bounced around impatiently. "Let's go!" she said.

 81

Gretchen skipped ahead and the others
followed. Everyone was feeling much
more cheery. Now there were four of
them working to save Patch!

CHAPTER TWO

A Thorny Trick

As they hurried along, Lily explained about the witch's spell.

"We must make the Rise and Shine potion, and give it to Patch before sunset," said Jess, "otherwise the poor little thing will sleep forever."

"Oh, that's so sad," said Gretchen,

stopping for a moment.

"We've already got one ingredient," said Poppy happily.

Gretchen smiled, "That's interesting, puppykins," she said. "Very interesting indeed. Where is it?"

"In Jess's pocket," said Poppy, dashing ahead impatiently. "Can we go on now?"

Gretchen skipped ahead, singing, "I love the flowers, I love the bees, I love butterflies with dusty knees…"

Lily and Jess grinned. "I think she loves the forest even more than we do," Lily whispered to her best friend.

"I wish she'd go faster," said Poppy, as Gretchen stopped by a ring of thick bushes covered in pale blue blossoms. "Oh no, she's smelling more flowers now. We'll never find that jewel water!"

But then Gretchen beckoned to them. "Come along, all of you." She pointed to the middle of the circle of bushes. "You'll find what you want in there. Go on," she said, "in you go."

"Thanks, Gretchen!" cried Jess, dashing into the centre. Lily and Poppy followed, then all three stood, looking and listening for the sound of water.

Jess turned to speak to Gretchen, who had stayed outside the flowery ring. *Why isn't she following us?* she wondered.

Lily was puzzled, too. "Gretchen, can you show—?" she began, then stopped as she realised Gretchen was speaking. No, not speaking – she was chanting!

"Branches twist in thorny curls,

Make a cage for nasty girls!"

At once, the bushes sent out hundreds of

thin, spidery branches that sprouted sharp

thorns, as long as sewing needles. The

branches twisted, curled and knotted until they were too dense to see through.

In no time at all, Jess, Lily and Poppy were surrounded by a thick, prickly cage!

"We're trapped!" cried Lily. "But why?"

"Gretchen, what have you done?" asked Jess, horrified.

The pretty face appeared above the spiky cage. Gretchen seemed to have grown taller. Then, to the girls' horror, yellow-green sparks crackled around her. The marmalade-coloured hair turned green, and the pretty dress became a swirling black cloak.

"It's Grizelda!" cried Lily. "Gretchen
was the witch in disguise. She's tricked us!"

Grizelda's awful cackle echoed round
the forest. "Haa haaa haaaa! You fools!
You're always visiting Toadstool Glade, so
I knew that if I waited there you'd show
up before long. And now you've told me
exactly what you're up to!"

Jess and Lily stared at her in horror.

The witch laughed again. "You won't find the jewel water, and you'll never find the Sunrise Berries. Even if you did, you'd never dare try to reach them. Haaa!"

She snapped her fingers and disappeared in a shower of evil-smelling yellow sparks.

Jess and Lily turned to comfort Poppy. The little puppy's eyes were brimming with tears. "We can't save Patch," she whimpered, "and we're trapped here. I'll never see my family again."

Lily picked her up and pressed her

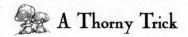

cheek against Poppy's. "Don't you worry,"
she said. "We've beaten Grizelda before
and we'll do it again. We'll think of
something," she added. "Won't we, Jess?"

Her friend put on a big smile. "Of course we will," she said.

But the girls exchanged nervous glances. It looked like Grizelda really had beaten them this time.

CHAPTER THREE

Desperate for Help

"I should have guessed there was something funny about Gretchen," Lily said with a sigh. "Goldie always said we're the only humans who can visit Friendship Forest. We should have been more careful."

Poppy put a paw into her hand. "It's

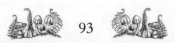

not your fault," she said.

"There is one good thing," Jess realised suddenly. "Grizelda's told us what the third ingredient is!"

"Sunrise Berries," said Lily. She glared at the thorny cage. "We could carry on searching, if we could just get out of here."

"But how?" Jess asked. "We've no scissors or—"

"Ssh!" said Poppy. Her ears pricked up.

"What can you hear?" asked Jess.

"Rustling," said Poppy. "Very close by."

Jess clenched her fists. "Not that witch again," she muttered.

"No," said Poppy. "It sounds like paws pattering… and squeaks…" She listened again, head on one side. "Mice!" she cried. "Maybe they can help!"

The girls leaped to their feet.

"Hey!" called Jess.

"Yap! Over here!" called Poppy.

"Behind the thorny bushes!" shouted Lily. She lay down on the ground and peered beneath the branches. "It's Molly Twinkletail!" she cried. "She must be on her way home from the Flower Festival." Lily cupped her hands to her mouth. "Molly! Over here!"

Jess bent down, too. "Her brothers and
sisters are with her," she said. "Molly!
We're trapped!"

Molly darted over and peered beneath
the bushes, then gasped in horror as she
saw the girls in the thorny cage.

"Please can you find someone to help
get us out?" asked Jess.

 96

Molly didn't reply. Instead, she looked thoughtful for a moment, then scampered to one of the twisted branches and bit it, hard. "No problem!" she said cheerily, and turned to her family. "Remember how Lily and Jess saved me when I was stuck behind that waterfall? Now we're going to save them! Come on, everyone. Nibble

 97

and bite for all you're worth!"

The mouse family set to work, using their sharp teeth to gnaw the branches. Nibble and bite, nibble and bite…

To their delight, Jess, Lily and Poppy watched a gap gradually begin to appear in the prickly cage. Soon, it was big enough for Poppy to squeeze through and escape. Not long after, Lily and Jess were free as well!

"Hooray!" cheered the Twinkletails.

Jess and Lily quickly explained about Patch and how they needed to make the Rise and Shine potion before sunset,

otherwise he would sleep forever, or
the Muddlepups would have to give up
Garden Grove and its healing plants to
Grizelda, so she could use them in her
horrid spells.

"We need to find jewel water," said Lily.
"We think it's from a stream with jewels
inside it."

The mice looked mystified. "I've never
seen anything like that in the forest."
Molly said sadly.

One of Molly's brothers, Nifty, said
shyly, "The plants here are big and lush
and very green, which usually means

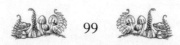

there's water nearby. If we can find the
water that makes these plants grow, we
might find the jewel water too."

"Oh, Nifty, you are clever!" said Lily,
blowing him a kiss.

His pink ears blushed bright red and he smiled happily.

Jess suggested they fan out in a circle to search. "Shout if you find water," she said.

Only minutes later, there was an excited squeak from Nifty at the edge of Toadstool Glade. He was spinning round and round, trying to grab his tail. Everyone ran over, wondering what he was doing.

Eventually, Nifty caught the end of his tail. "Look!" he squeaked.

Jess and Lily peered closely.

"Water," said Jess. "Water droplets on Nifty's tail!" She felt the grass. It was damp.

Then Poppy sniffed and padded to a patch of soft green ferns. "Here!" she cried, bouncing in excitement. "Water! Over here! We've found it!"

CHAPTER FOUR:

Bottle Blooms

Lily ran to hold the ferns aside. A silvery spring bubbled up from the earth into a trickle no wider than her hand. There, glittering in the sparkling little stream, were brightly coloured jewels. The water flowing over them sparkled with all the colours of the rainbow.

 103

Lily scooped some up into her hands and it twinkled in her palms.

"Jewel water!" cried Jess, leaning over her shoulder. "It definitely looks magical, doesn't it?"

Lily let it run through her fingers, then she and Jess grabbed each other and jumped up and down, with Poppy bounding around them.

"It's the second ingredient!" Lily cried. "Well done, Poppy!" She turned to the mouse family. "Thank you, Twinkletails. We wouldn't be here if it wasn't for your sharp teeth – and Nifty's tail!"

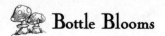

The little mice scampered around their feet, squeaking happily.

Once they had recovered from their excitement, Jess said, "We have to take the water to Patch. But we haven't got a bucket. How can we carry it?"

Poppy's tail started wagging. "Bottle blooms!" she cried, and began searching inside her flower bag. She pulled out a bunch of pale, bottle-shaped

blue flowers. "They never spill a drop,"
Poppy explained. "We can use them to
carry the jewel water."

Lily and Jess held the
bottle blooms steady
while the Twinkletails
filled their baskets
from the spring, then
carefully poured the
shimmering water
into the flowers. Poppy
showed the girls how

to twist the tiny petals at the top of the
flowers to seal them closed.

"Thank goodness for your flower bag, Poppy," said Lily, as she and Jess tucked the bottle blooms safely into their pockets.

"Now to find the Sunrise Berries," said Jess. "Molly, have you ever seen them on the menu at the Toadstool Café?"

Molly and her family shook their heads. "I've never seen them on the Treasure Tree either," said Nifty. "That's where most of our food comes from."

"It's really tall, though," said Molly, "the tallest tree in the forest. I don't think anyone has explored all of it."

Jess noticed that Lily was frowning

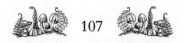

107

slightly. "What's wrong?" she asked.

"I was thinking," said Lily, "that maybe the clue is in the name. Sunrise Berries. Anything growing right at the top of the Treasure Tree would be first to see the sunrise. Maybe that's where we'll find them."

Jess gave a whoop of delight. "I bet you're right," she cried. "Thanks, Twinkletails. We're off to explore the Treasure Tree!"

CHAPTER FIVE

The Treasure Tree

The Treasure Tree was huge, so big that when Lily looked up it seemed to fill the sky. Food hung from its branches and long vines dangled around the trunk. Poppy told the girls to each tie a vine around their waist. Then she clambered up onto Lily's back.

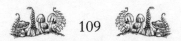

"Now pull
the vines," said Poppy.

Lily and Jess gave them a tug. To their
amazement, they were lifted off the
ground!

The vines pulled them gently up
through the branches. Poppy held tight,
ducking whenever a melon or a bunch of
bananas threatened to bump into her.

They passed clumps of every sort of
nut, even coconuts, and they could smell
the sweet strawberry branch

long before they
reached it.

Jess's mouth watered
when she saw fat
purple plums. She was
just about to pick one,
when she heard a voice
above her.

"Ssh!" she whispered
to the others. "Someone's
singing up there."

Lily felt her tummy tighten. "Not Gretchen, I hope," she whispered. She stretched upwards to look, and jumped as a furry tail swished by.

The voice sang, "Nuts, nuts, I'm nuts about nuts…"

"It's Woody Flufftail!" cried Poppy. "Hey, Woody!"

Lily and Jess gave their vines another tug to make them stop, and stepped onto one of the branches. The squirrel's cute little face peeped between two golden pineapples.

"Hello, Poppy! Hello, Jess and Lily!" he

chattered. "Wasn't the Flower Festival fun?
I'm collecting apricots for a pie. What are
you looking for?"

"Sunrise Berries," said Poppy. She
explained about Patch and the potion.
"We think the berries might grow at the
top of the Treasure Tree, and we need
them badly."

"They could be up there," agreed
Woody, "but I've heard they're very rare."

He leaped onto the trunk. "Follow me,"
he cried. "If there are any Sunrise Berries
up there, I'll find them!"

He bounded up through the branches,
his fluffy tail rippling. The others followed
on their vines. When they reached the top,
Lily, Jess and Poppy stared in wonder at
the great forest spread out beneath them.

"What an amazing sight," said Lily.

"Forget the view," said Jess. "Let's look
for Sunrise Berries."

They scanned the topmost branches.
Tucked among the tree's thick green
leaves were peanuts and peaches, lemons

and limes, gooseberries and grapefruits, but no Sunrise Berries.

"Sorry, everyone," Woody said sadly. "I wish I could have helped you."

Lily sat down on a branch, hugging the tearful Poppy. "We must have got it wrong," the puppy wailed, "thinking the berries would grow at the top of the tallest tree."

"No, it was a good idea," said Woody. "They do grow high up. It's just unlucky that the Treasure Tree doesn't have any growing right now."

"But there's no taller tree in the forest than this one," said Lily. "So where else

could they be?"

Jess felt a chill as she glanced around again, this time looking even further than the forest's edge.

Far off, across dark water, stood a cold, forbidding tower. Grey clouds hung above it, and Jess jumped as a bolt of

lightning lit up the building's roof. She squinted and could just about make out the shape of a woman at the window – a woman with tendrils of long, green hair.

"Grizelda!" Jess gasped. "That horrid tower must be her home." She shivered. "Remember what she said – that we'd never *dare* try to reach the berries?"

Lily felt her heart sink as she nodded. "Maybe the Berries are high up. But

instead of being up a tree…"

"…they're at the top of Grizelda's tower," finished Jess grimly. "I'm afraid it makes sense."

Lily felt close to tears as she stroked Poppy. "Let's go back down," she said.

They said goodbye to Woody and the vines gently lowered them back through the branches. Poppy clung onto Lily's back, paws around her neck.

On the ground, poor Poppy's ears drooped miserably. Her eyes were wet with tears. "We'll never save Patch," she sobbed. "Not if the Sunrise Berries are at the top of the witch's tower. No one would dare to go there."

Lily and Jess looked at each other.

"We dare," said Jess in the bravest voice she could muster.

"That's right," said Lily. "It'll be OK, Poppy. Think about what we've done already! We found out about the potion, we escaped from that nasty cage, and we've found the first two ingredients. And we couldn't have done all that without you!"

"Exactly," said Jess. "Now we're going to the witch's tower and we're going to get those berries."

Poppy's tail started to wag. "And then we'll save Patch!" she said.

"We will," said Jess firmly.

The girls shared a smile. They didn't know if they'd manage to beat Grizelda, but they were sure of one thing – they would never stop trying!

Story Three
Sunrise Berries

CHAPTER ONE: A Ride to the Tower   123

CHAPTER TWO: A Frightening Climb   135

CHAPTER THREE: The Black Vine   145

CHAPTER FOUR: Back to the Den   153

CHAPTER FIVE: Goodbye, Muddlepups! 163

CHAPTER ONE

A Ride to the Tower

The sun was already low in the sky by the time Lily Hart, Jess Forester and Poppy Muddlepup the puppy made it to the other side of Friendship Forest. The three friends stood by a stretch of still, dark water at the forest's edge, staring at the witch Grizelda's stone tower on the far

side. It stood on ground that was strangely
rocky and grey, and studded with bare,
black bushes. The tower loomed over the
water, tall and creepy-looking. Yellow-
green sparks shot out of the top.

They had already collected two of
the ingredients they needed
for the Rise and Shine
potion – a tiny feather
and some jewel water.
The final ingredient
was Sunrise Berries.

They had until sunset to find them and
then mix up the potion to wake Poppy's
brother Patch from his enchanted sleep.
If they failed, Grizelda would wake
him, but only in return for keeping all
the magical flowers in the Muddlepups'
Garden Grove for herself. These plants
were needed to heal all the poorly
animals in Friendship Forest, and
the Muddlepup family were their
special guardians.

   "The berries must be at

the top of the tower somewhere," said Jess, summoning all her courage. *I hope those sparks don't mean Grizelda is practising her witchy magic,* she thought nervously to herself.

"So let's go and get them!" said Lily, setting off. But then she groaned. "Oh no! How are we going to get across the water?"

"Perhaps there's a bridge or stepping stones," Poppy suggested. "Or even a boat. Let's look!"

They began searching along the bank. Poppy raced ahead, but after a minute or two there was a sharp "Yap!" and she bounded back. Her tail wagged so fast it was a blur, just like Honey Needlenose's hummingbird wings.

"There are some frogs just up ahead," said Poppy. "They say they'll help us. Come on!"

Jess and Lily followed, wondering how on earth frogs could help them cross the water. But when they reached them, they could see at once! The frogs were sitting on huge, round lily pads, the biggest and flattest the girls had ever seen. They floated on the water like giant tea trays. In the middle of each lily pad was a little

hut, and outside each hut were frogs of all
shapes and sizes.

The biggest frog, who carried a fishing
net on a stick, called, "Hello, we're the
Greenhop family. Poppy says you need
help, so hop, hop, hop aboard!" He turned
to his family. "Grab your oars, everyone.
To the horrible witch's tower!"

Lily, Jess and Poppy each chose a lily
pad and carefully stepped onto it. It felt

very wobbly. Water trickled over the
edges, so the girls sat right in the middle,
hugging their knees. Poppy climbed onto
Mr Greenhop's lily pad, then put her head
down with her paws over her eyes and
her tail pointing straight up in the air.

The frogs got out their oars, and off they rowed, gliding over the dark water. Mr Greenhop swung his net in the air every so often.

"I'm catching flies," he explained. "Lots of flies around the witch's home."

Soon they reached the far bank. Lily shivered as she looked at the tower.

"Hop, hop, hop ashore," whispered Mr Greenhop. "I don't want to stay on this side for too long – we're far too close to that witch for my liking!"

Lily, Jess and Poppy thanked the Greenhops for their help, and stepped

onto the bank. Now they knew why they
were shivering, and why the ground was
grey. On Grizelda's side of the water, it was
winter! Snow lay on the ground, but not
crisp and white, as it was in Brightley. This
was dirty grey and slushy.

"Everything about Grizelda's
tower is horrible," muttered
Jess. "Even the snow."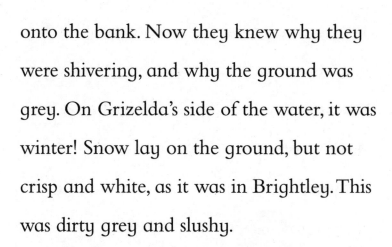

"I wish we had our
jackets and scarves
back," Lily said with
a shiver.

"Wait!" said

Poppy. She pulled three red flowers with sparkling centres from her bag. "Winter warmers," she explained. "If you have one of these on you, it keeps you nice and toasty warm."

Lily and Jess each tucked a winter warmer into their hair, where the twisting twirls were before, while Poppy looped hers through her bandana.

"Wow," gasped Lily, as she felt a lovely

heat surround through her. "Your flowers really are magical, Poppy!"

Jess led the way between spiteful-looking thorn bushes, which seemed to reach out and snatch at their clothes. A big, ugly, warty toad waddled out in front of Poppy and swelled up, making the poor puppy jump. Lily flapped her hands at the toad, then picked Poppy up.

"This place smells mean and nasty," said the puppy, wrinkling her nose.

As they reached the tower, Lily gazed upwards. "Wow! It's so tall," she said.

The walls were black and crumbling in

places, and the narrow windows were as
dark and cold as the witch's eyes.

Jess gasped and pointed. A black vine
had wound its way around the very
top of the tower. Growing on it was
something bright, sparkling and orange.
"Sunrise Berries!" she said.

Poppy wriggled in excitement.

"See?" said Lily. "Everything will be
fine. We're going to save Patch."

"There's only one problem," Jess
muttered. "We have to get to the top of
the tower – without being spotted by
Grizelda!"

CHAPTER TWO

A Frightening Climb

Jess found a door in the tower wall. It was big and solid, and had a knocker shaped like a scary monster face. Lily and Poppy kept close behind her as she reached for the iron doorknob. Everyone held their breath nervously. . .

But it wouldn't turn.

"It's locked," said Jess. "Now what?"

"Keep looking for a way in," said Lily.

They tiptoed around the outside of
the tower, then Poppy gave a little yap.
"There's an open window," she said, "but
it's too high up, even for you girls."

Jess groaned but Lily had an idea.

"Keep watch, Poppy," said Lily. "Jess
and I will find something to stand on."

Poppy sat beneath the window, her ears
pricked, watching for danger. Lily and Jess
soon found what they needed – a rotten
tree stump that had been ripped from
the ground. They dragged it to the wall

and stood it in the grey slush
beneath the window.

Jess climbed onto the
stump and reached up to
the window. In moments
she had hauled herself over
the sill and inside. She
looked out. "Pass Poppy
up to me," she told Lily.

Once the puppy was lifted through the open window, she immediately sneezed. "Ooh, it's dusty," she complained, rubbing her nose with a paw.

"Let's be as quiet as we can!" Jess whispered. "Lily, your turn now. Stand on the stump and stretch your arms. Grab my wrists!"

Seconds later, Lily stood beside Jess, brushing down her dress.

"Careful," Poppy whispered. "All this dust is very sneezy."

They found themselves in a damp, dark hallway. It smelled of mould, and musty, stale air. In the corner was a stone spiral staircase. When they stood at the bottom and looked up, it seemed to go all the way up through the tower.

"Come on," said Jess, leading the way up the stairs. Cobwebs brushed their hair, and each footstep stirred more dust. Poppy was right. It was very sneezy!

The puppy's ears suddenly pricked up. "Listen!" she said.

"What is it?" asked Lily.

"Footsteps," whispered Poppy. "Grizelda's coming!"

"Oh no," said Lily. "Hide! Quick!"

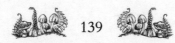

Jess spotted a door, covered in sagging spiders' webs. She wrenched it open and saw it was a cupboard, full of huge old iron cauldrons.

Jess, Lily and Poppy darted inside, shutting the door softly behind them. And not a moment too soon! Seconds later, through the gaps in the wood, they saw Grizelda climbing down the stairs. She was carrying a lantern and crowing to herself.

"It'll soon be sunset, haa haa!" she said. "Those interfering girls will never be able to make the potion in time, even if they do find all the ingredients. The magic plants will be mine – all of them. Haaaaaa, haaaa, haaa!"

As she stomped past, the thick dust on the cauldrons filled the air, billowing up around the girls and Poppy. The puppy's paw flew to her nose.

"Oh no!" whispered Lily. She guessed

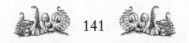

there was a sneeze coming and quickly wrapped the puppy in her arms, hoping to stifle the sound.

"Aaah… aah… aah…" Poppy managed to hold back the sneeze for a moment, but then—"Fwooff!"

Through the gaps in the door, Jess saw the wicked witch stop.

"Who's there?" Grizelda snapped.

"Quick!" whispered Lily. "Hide in one of the big cauldrons."

They clambered inside the largest one, hardly daring to breathe.

"Who's there, I say?" snarled Grizelda.

"Show yourself or I'll... Aha! The cupboard!"

Lily, still hugging Poppy, could feel the pup's heart racing as fast as her own.

Grizelda yanked the door open. Shadows moved as the witch swung the lantern forward.

On the wall, Jess saw the silhouette

of witchy hair, swirling like snakes as
Grizelda peered into the cupboard.

Oh no, Jess thought. *Please, please don't
let her see us!*

CHAPTER THREE

The Black Vine

Jess's legs were like cotton wool, and Lily clapped her hand over her mouth to stop herself crying out. Both girls felt Poppy's little body trembling between them.

Grizelda's lantern swung closer. If she came any nearer, she would see them! The girls held their breath for what felt

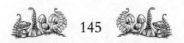

like forever before Grizelda grunted.

"Humph. It must have been a rat."

The girls breathed again as the door slammed shut and Grizelda's voice faded away, muttering, "If I catch anyone…"

They waited a few moments to be sure she had gone, then Jess climbed out of the cauldron and opened the door. "That was close!" she said. "Come on – let's get those berries and get out of here!"

The others followed, hurrying up the stairs after her.

Both girls pulled sticky cobwebs from their faces as they climbed, and they had to watch where they stepped. Some of the worn stairs were slippery with puddles of green, slimy water.

At last they reached a small wooden door. There was nowhere else to go, so Jess pushed it open, and they found themselves in a courtyard on the tower's roof.

It was a relief to be in the fresh, cold air, but a horrible smell wafted across to them, like rotten eggs soaked in stagnant pond water. It came from a fountain of dirty water that sent puffs of yellow-green sparks up into the air.

Beyond the fountain was a black vine.

Poppy Muddlepup

"Look!" cried Jess in delight.

All along the vine, brilliant orange berries

sparkled in the rays of the setting sun.

Lily clapped her hands with glee and

Poppy let out a yap of delight. The three

friends made their way past the fountain.

"Be careful not to let any droplets touch

you," Lily warned. "Grizelda's

bad magic could be in that

stinky water."

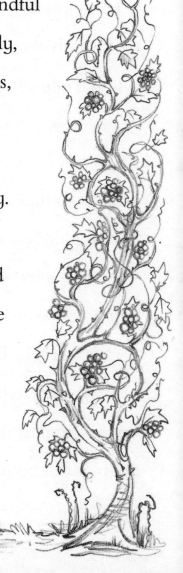

When they reached the vine, Jess
reached out to grab a handful
of the berries. Immediately,
there was a flash of sparks,
and jagged shards of ice
appeared on the berries,
covering them completely.

"Oh no!" cried Jess.
"Grizelda knows we need
the berries. She must have
put a spell on them, in
case we managed to

escape from that horrible cage."

Lily picked up a stone from the ground and smashed it onto one of the frozen shards. But instead of shattering, more sparks fizzed from the ice. They all took a step back.

Worry swirled inside Jess. "What are we going to do?" she asked.

Poppy's ears pricked up and she gave a yap. "The winter warmers!"

"Yes!" cried Lily. "Oh, you clever puppy."

They each held their winter warmer flowers against the ice. As the heat from the blooms spread, drips began to splatter on the ground.

"The ice is melting!" said Lily.

Soon, the girls were able to grab handfuls of the velvety berries. Lily stuffed them into her pocket.

Jess looked up at the sky. The light was growing dim. "It's almost sunset," she said, turning to Lily. "How will we get back to the Muddlepups' den in time?"

"Oh no!" wailed Poppy. "We've got everything we need, but we're too late to save poor Patch." She put her paws over her eyes and sobbed.

"Oh, Poppy, we're so sorry!" said Jess,

blinking back her own tears as she hugged the shaking puppy. "We did everything we could. Grizelda was just too clever for us."

"Wait! Listen!" said Lily. "What's that? I heard a voice!"

Jess and Poppy turned, expecting to see Grizelda. But it wasn't the witch!

"Look, Jess!" she cried.

Captain Ace, the stork, was flying towards them with a rope in his long beak, pulling his hot air balloon along.

And in the balloon's basket was Goldie!

CHAPTER FOUR

Back to the Den

"Goldie!" cried Jess. "How did you know where we were?"

Ace lowered the basket to the tower roof, and Goldie sprang out. She hugged her friends, and cuddled Poppy. Then she quickly told them how she'd found them.

"When I got back to Friendship Forest

 153

after visiting Barney," she explained, "I found Mrs Taptree waiting for me. She told me about poor Patch and the potion and rushed me to Garden Grove. Then Woody Flufftail came by and said you had two ingredients already and were looking for Sunrise Berries."

"We found them," said Lily. "Right here in Grizelda's tower!"

"I guessed you would," said Goldie. "You're brave and clever, and I knew you'd do your best to find all the things you needed."

"And you found us!" said Jess.

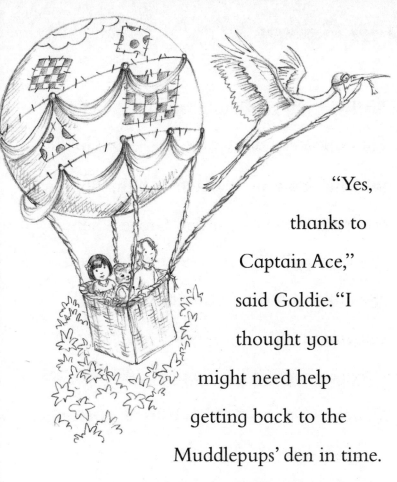

"Yes, thanks to Captain Ace," said Goldie. "I thought you might need help getting back to the Muddlepups' den in time. Now quick – into the basket!"

When they were all safely aboard, Ace flew them away and over the forest. As the balloon took them further and further from Grizelda's chilly tower, they felt happier and happier. But then Goldie gasped. "Hurry!" she cried. "The sun has almost set!"

Captain Ace's wings beat harder and the balloon moved faster through the darkening sky.

Poppy spotted her family's den first. "There, Captain Ace!" she cried, pointing her paw.

Ace lowered the balloon over the den and Lily climbed down a rope ladder, being careful not to step on the magical flowers below. Who knew what might happen if they were trodden on?

Jess passed Poppy to Lily, then she and Goldie climbed down.

Everyone yelled, "Thank you!" to Captain Ace as he flew off with the balloon. Then they rushed into the den, calling, "We're back!"

Mr and Mrs Muddlepup were sitting with Patch, who was still fast asleep in his nest of blankets. They looked very worried.

"Poppy, fetch a bowl, please," Lily said. Then she explained their plan to the Muddlepups, "We're going to make the

Rise and Shine potion, and then we're going to wake Patch up."

Jess carefully emptied the jewel water out of the bottle blooms and into the bowl, then Lily dropped in the berries and added the hummingbird feather.

There was a *fizzle!* and a *pffft!* as the ingredients dissolved into a swirling, foaming, orange mixture. It began to glow with magic.

"It's turning as bright as the sunrise," Lily said. "That's a good sign, isn't it?" she asked anxiously.

No one replied. Lily guessed that they were all wondering the same thing. *Oh please let the potion work*, she thought desperately.

Mrs Muddlepup propped Patch up. Lily took a spoon and carefully dripped a little of the potion into his mouth. She'd done this sort of thing with medicine many times before at the wildlife hospital,

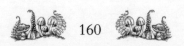

but she'd never been quite so nervous.

The potion fizzed as it touched Patch's tongue. His mouth moved a little as he tasted it. Now Lily was able to give him a whole spoonful.

Fizzle… fizzle, it went.

Patch's nose twitched. He yawned a great wide yawn. And finally – he opened his eyes!

Mrs Muddlepup burst into happy tears. "You've saved him! Oh, thank you, girls, you've saved my little Patch! How can we ever repay you?"

Jess and Lily felt as if they would

160

explode with pleasure and relief. Through
the windows, they could just see the
last rays of the setting sun lighting the
magical grove. They'd been just in time!

But then Jess saw something else.

 161

An orb of eerie yellow-green light was
floating down towards the Muddlepups'
cosy den.

"Grizelda!" cried Jess. "She's coming!"

CHAPTER FIVE

Goodbye, Muddlepups!

Goldie and the girls hurried out and saw the orb explode in a shower of evil-smelling sparks. There stood Grizelda, her dark eyes glittering coldly.

"This is it!" the witch sneered. "Your last chance to save Patch. Hand over Garden Grove and the magical plants

 163

to me, and the puppy will wake. If you refuse, he will sleep forever! Haaa!" Her laugh boomed like thunder.

Lily and Jess heard movement behind them and turned to see the Muddlepups emerging from their den. Last to come out was Patch – looking as wide awake and bouncy as ever! Grizelda gasped when she saw the puppy. A look of fury spread across her face, and her wild green hair stood out like the bristles on a hairbrush.

"How did this happen?" she shrieked. "You couldn't have made the Rise and Shine potion, because you didn't have all the ingredients!" She pointed at Patch. "He broke my spell! How did he break it? Answer me!"

Jess went to speak, but Goldie hushed her. "Grizelda doesn't know you got the Sunrise Berries from her tower," she whispered. "She thinks Patch has special magic powers!"

Jess's face lit up. "Let's tell her that

all the Muddlepups are magical," she whispered back, "and that she'd better leave them alone if she knows what's good for her."

Lily nodded and turned to the Muddlepups so that her back was to Grizelda, putting a finger to her lips.

Jess spoke in a loud voice. "Of course Patch broke your spell. Everyone knows that all the Muddlepups are magical and can break spells. Isn't that right, Lily?"

"Yes, that's why they look after Garden Grove," Lily said. "They have special powers, so you'd better stay away,

Grizelda! There are four of them and there's only one of you!"

Jess glanced around. The Muddlepups were trying to hide their grins.

"I'm magical, too, you horrible witch!" Poppy shouted bravely. She skittered past the girls, clutching a handful of purple pompom puffballs. She held them up and chanted nonsense words. "Bikker cree duckfar!" Then she blew on them, releasing clouds of bright pink

167

smoke, just as she had shown the girls
earlier. It wafted towards the witch.

"Run, Grizelda!" Lily called. "Poppy
just did a spell that makes witches
disappear!"

Grizelda screamed and backed away
from the pink cloud. "You might have
won this time," she shrieked, "but this isn't
the last you'll see of me!"

She snapped her fingers and vanished
in a shower of yellow sparks.

After a moment's silence, everyone burst
into loud cheers. "Hooray!"

Mr and Mrs Muddlepup hugged the

 168

girls, and both their tails wagged madly.

"We're not really magical, are we?" asked Patch. "We're not special?"

Lily smiled. "We did make up most of what we said to fool Grizelda," she explained, "but you Muddlepups definitely are special."

"And so are you girls!" yapped Poppy in delight.

A little while later, they were all enjoying Mrs Muddlepup's delicious sweetroot soup and hazelnut crackers, and then it was time for Jess and Lily to say goodbye. There were lots of hugs

169

for everyone, and kisses and cuddles for Poppy, then Goldie took the Lily and Jess all the way back to the Friendship Tree. The girls put their warm clothes back on while Goldie touched a paw to the trunk.

"Thank you for helping with the flower

festival," she said as the door appeared,
"and thanks for helping the Muddlepups."

They both hugged her.

"I'll come and visit you again," Goldie
promised.

"I hope it will be soon," said Lily.

"Me, too!" said Jess. "Bye, Goldie." She
opened the door and stepped into the
shimmering golden light.

Lily followed and both girls found
themselves back in Brightley Meadow.
Snow was falling softly, sparkling white.
It was nothing like the dirty grey slush
around Grizelda's tower.

"Let's hurry back," said Jess. "That hot chocolate will be waiting!" The girls knew that no time passed in the human world while they were in Friendship Forest.

They raced across the meadow, over the stream, and up the garden until they reached the woodpeckers' aviary. They crept inside the enclosure and quietly lifted the nest box lid. The chicks were snuggled together, fast asleep.

"Aah, they're just like Dig and Tipper," said Lily.

"But quieter!" giggled Jess.

In the kitchen, Mrs Hart passed them

172

steaming mugs of hot chocolate with pink marshmallows. "You'd never guess what I just saw," she said. "Ollie was walking his dog, and a beautiful golden cat walked right alongside it, almost as if they were friends!"

Lily and Jess shared a secret smile. That golden cat was their friend, too. Their magical friend! They couldn't wait for their next adventure with Goldie in Friendship Forest!

The End

Magic
Animal Friends

Look out for the brand-new
Magic Animal Friends series,
coming soon!

Series Two

www.magicanimalfriends.com

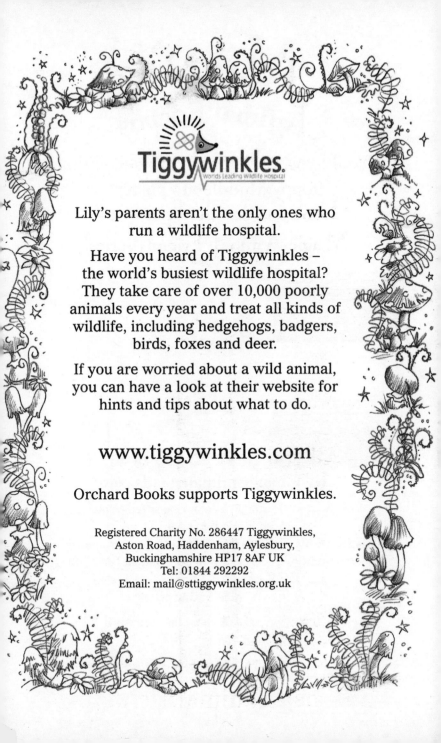

Tiggywinkles.
Worlds Leading Wildlife Hospital

Lily's parents aren't the only ones who run a wildlife hospital.

Have you heard of Tiggywinkles – the world's busiest wildlife hospital? They take care of over 10,000 poorly animals every year and treat all kinds of wildlife, including hedgehogs, badgers, birds, foxes and deer.

If you are worried about a wild animal, you can have a look at their website for hints and tips about what to do.

www.tiggywinkles.com

Orchard Books supports Tiggywinkles.

Registered Charity No. 286447 Tiggywinkles,
Aston Road, Haddenham, Aylesbury,
Buckinghamshire HP17 8AF UK
Tel: 01844 292292
Email: mail@sttiggywinkles.org.uk

Magic
Animal Friends

Would you like to win a limited edition
Poppy Muddlepup poster?

All you have to do is visit
www.magicanimalfriends.com

join the club, download a colouring sheet, colour it in
and send it to us at…

Magic Animal Friends Poppy Muddlepup Competition
Orchard Books, 338 Euston Road, London, NW1 3BH
We will put all entries into a draw for the chance
to win this amazing prize!

Prize draws will take place on the 30th April 2015
and 31st July 2015

Competition open only to UK and Republic of Ireland residents.
No purchase necessary. For full terms and conditions please go to
www.hachettechildrens.co.uk/terms

Good Luck!